THE ARRANGEMENT 18
THE FERRO FAMILY

BY:

H.M. WARD

www.SexyAwesomeBooks.com

COPYRIGHT

H.M. WARD PRESS
First Edition: February 2015
ISBN: 9781630350642

THE ARRANGEMENT 18

Dear Reader,

The Arrangement Series is different. How? The story is organic—and growing swiftly. Originally intended to be four serial novels, fans of the series demanded more Sean & Avery, spurring an entirely new concept: a fan-driven series. When fans ask for more, I write more.

I am astonished and humbled by the response this series has received. As the series grows, I am constantly fascinated by the requests and insights from readers. This series has sold over 4 MILLION copies! The average length of each book is 125 pages in paperback and can be read in a few hours or less.

This series intertwines with my other work, but is designed to be read independently, as a quick read between other titles.

You can join in the discussion via my Facebook page: www.facebook.com/AuthorHMWard.

For a complete listing of Ferro books, look here: www.SexyAwesomeBooks.com & click BOOKS.

Thank you and happy reading!

~Holly

Chapter 1

Sean towers above me, his toned body backlit by the chandelier hanging overhead. If he'd said anything else, I would have thought he was an angel in that moment. Repeating the phrase, he kneels down and whispers, "You shouldn't have come."

There's not a drop of strength left in my body. I can't fathom why Sean answered the door in the first place. Where's Jeeves or whatever they call him? He's Constance's right arm. That guy was supposed to take me to the craziest Ferro of them all. That would have worked. I had to choose a side, and it's clear that I didn't pick Sean.

Even so, Sean moves closer, trailing his fingers along my temple, and smearing through the blood staining my skin. Those blue eyes pin me in place. I can't move, or speak. I can't tell him why I'm here or what I intended to do, although I suspect that he already knows. Those luscious lips of his are smooth and his jaw isn't locked tight.

I must be delirious. Why isn't he mad?

He whispers again, "Why do you do this to me? It's like you decided to make my life a living hell from day one."

That's rich, I made his life hell. "Are we talking proximity or prostitution? Because I sure as hell never thought I'd be this close to a Ferro, or spread my legs for one, ever again." I'm taunting him, pressing buttons that will set him off. I can't help it, my defenses are up.

Sean makes a deep sound in the back of his throat and cocks his head to the side. "Irony."

"Ain't that the truth."

"Stop speaking like a hillbilly. You know how lusty that makes me." Sean's lips twitch as if he's trying not to laugh.

He should be mad, but he's not. I don't get it.

Holding up a finger, I wave it between us and then press it to his nose. Those cobalt eyes remain locked on mine, ignoring my touch. "Boop."

"Oh God. Was this your plan? To come to the mansion and boop my mother on the nose?" He laughs, amused for real. Sean shakes his head, like I'm a pathologically needy black hole—I suck everyone and everything into my mess of a life, if they get too close. Sean's been sitting on the edge, carefully balancing himself—until now. His demeanor shifts as he scoops me up into his arms.

"Where are we going?" I thought this was his bedroom.

Sean's hand covers my lips, silencing me. "Shhh. I don't want them to hear you." With that, Sean turns on his heel and retreats, taking me from this room, and carries me into a darkened hallway.

My eyelids feel like lead and I can't help it, they droop as my cheek falls against his chest. I finally ask, "You're not mad?"

Sean is quiet and then smiles. "No."

"I came to your mother instead of you. You know what that means. Right?" I should probably shut up now, but I can't.

He nods once, carefully, as he pads down hall after hall. We pass no one, which is odd. No maids, no servants of any kind.

Sean sucks in air and glances down at me. "I did the same thing, thinking it would save you. I can only imagine what you thought the Ice Queen could do. Mother has a way of overpromising and under delivering. For example, she promised me a particular name the night of Trystan's concert, and I promised her something in return."

His voice trails off as we come to a set of massive wooden doors. They tower above us and each panel is carved intricately and laced with iron. There's iron lattice work, scrolls, and twisting decorative bars.

I reach out, sliding the pads of my fingers over a piece of metal. "Was this on purpose? All the iron? An old lady told me that Ferro means iron in Italian."

Sean smiles. "I'm not certain. Mother didn't elaborate whether it was a preference for the Old World style or family pride. Either way, I'm glad you like it, because my rooms are nothing but wood and iron."

My heart turns to ice and drops to my toes. "Your rooms?"

Sean nods, sensing my reaction. He tightens his hold on me, and repeats those words once more, "You shouldn't have come."

Chapter 2

The interior of the Ferro mansion is a labyrinth. I couldn't find the front door again if I tried, and Sean's rooms don't appear to have another exit, aside from the massive double doors. I struggle to get out of his arms. Between his cryptic words and the serene look on his face, I'm more than mortified.

Swallowing hard, I ask, "I didn't think you lived here anymore."

"I don't." Sean continues walking with me cradled against his chest, passing from one lavish room to the next. His rooms are dark red, gold, and filled with leather and iron. Each velvet drape hangs from twenty feet up and extends all the way down to the floor. They're closed, sealing out the light. Golden tassels adorn the pillows on a brown leather Tantra Chair. Leather cords are wrapped around the legs and tucked neatly underneath. It's the only piece of furniture in this room.

My jaw drops and I stare at it. Sean notices, "When I turned twenty-one I was given funds to redecorate my quarters. This is my favorite room, although the box is long gone."

I stare at the chaise lounge and stiffen in his arms. The memories of the box come racing back, making me shiver in a bad way, and then my stomach twists as if disappointed. What the hell is wrong with me? I didn't like the box.

"Poor little rich boy only got a sex room for his birthday." I make a pouty face, but I can't hold it in place. When we enter the next room, the ceilings stretch higher. Ornate moldings, covered in gold, accent the deep red finish on the walls. Golden drapes cover these windows, but they are pulled back enough to let in a little bit of light. That sliver of light lands directly on the biggest bed I've ever seen in my life. It's the size of two king beds pushed together.

The burgundy crushed silk coverlet lies over a fluffy down comforter. Tall spires of iron and wood stretch into the air, the tops adorned with swags of cream and blood red silk. They tangle together and hang down the poles, forming puddles of fabric.

An antique carpet covers a hand carved floor that looks an awful lot like ebony. I can only imagine how much the floor alone cost. As I look around, my senses are filled with things that are rich and lavish. Dark bookcases line another wall. They also appear to be custom and hand carved. The Ferro family crest adorns the top of each case. It's inlaid with gold filigree on the center bookcase, surrounded by red stones that I can only assume are rubies. This is more opulent than I would've ever thought. The ceiling is obviously 24 karat gold leaf. I can see each little patch and know someone took hours upon hours applying each one by hand. Over the years, it's developed a beautiful finish.

Opposite the bed are more large iron doors with ornate twisting metal, inlaid with mirrors so I can't see what's beyond.

"Would you believe me if I said I've never done more than sleep in here?" Sean smirks and gently sets me down on his bed.

"Liar." I try to tease, to smile, but I'm pretty sure I look like I've been dragged through the Pine Barrens after falling off a donkey. I'm schmexy.

Sean leans over me, allowing those dark eyes to move from cut to cut. When he gets to the ones on my hands, he lifts my wrists and looks closer. "And why would I lie about it, Miss Smith? Especially when you are laying here in obvious distress on my bed?"

A smile crosses my lips. "You sleep here?"

"When I sleep, yes. And if I owe my mother a favor, I tend to stay close by."

"What favor do you owe her?"

His dark lashes lower and he glances to the side after dropping my wrist. "I promised her that I'd get rid of you."

Chapter 3

Jerking upright, I'm ready to bolt from the room, but Sean steps in front of me. Grabbing my shoulders, he stops me. "Stop and listen before you make any decisions. Avery, trust me here."

I laugh bitterly. "You lied to me, abused me, bought me, sold me, and trapped me. Did I leave anything out?"

"Yeah, one important thing—I saved you. I bartered for your life. I promised to get rid of you if Mother gave me the name of the person trying to gun us down. I'd assumed it was me they were after. I assumed too many things, and since I had no other options, I agreed. The problem came when I learned the gunners name was Marty. I backed him into a corner one day and that's how we ended up working together. He wouldn't let them hurt you— the dumb ass fell in love with his mark." Sean smirks. His hands trail down my arms as he stares at me. "I can't say I blame him."

"So, you reneged on a promise to your evil Mother?" He nods. I feel sick. I was gonna come here and ask Constance for help, meanwhile she was trying to think of ways to get me chopped up and shipped away. It makes me wonder why he'd cross his mother and I can't help it, I have to ask, "Why?"

"Why do you think?" I'm not sure, but I don't say it. I still don't know if he's being friendly, or poising me so he can inflict the most damage.

When I don't answer, Sean continues. "Masterson might have been an asshole for falling for you, but I was worse. I trusted Black to give me a girl I could handle. I thought you'd come one night, and be gone the next morning. But, things didn't work out that way. Now, I can't stand the thought of seeing you leave. I'm too late. I already know that. I did too much, and went too far. I don't expect anything from you. But, if you'll let me, I'll get you to safety and you won't be alone."

My brows scrunch together. "You're sending me away with a blind date? How nice of you." Sarcasm drips from my voice. This is not what I want to hear.

Sean is being uncommonly kind, especially for him. "Avery, this isn't the time to argue. Besides, you two are good for each other."

"Ahhh," I nod, catching his meaning, "Trystan. You think I belong with him."

"He's the safer choice." Sean seems serious when he says it, like he thinks I actually have a better shot with Trystan than with him.

It makes me irate but I temper my rage, holding it just below the surface. "I don't understand. You'd rather see me in the arms of another man?"

"No," his voice is barely a whisper, and sounds almost like a confession. "But I messed up too many times, and I keep telling you that I can't be the guy you want—the guy you need. Trystan can. He's going to ask you—"

"Shut up about Trystan. He's not the one I want. I want you."

Sean steps away and shakes his head. "It's too late."

"It's never too late. I do anything and everything, for a price. Remember, Mr. Jones?" My voice is even, confident. A pen and pad of paper catch my eye. I pace over to them and scrawl my terms onto the pad. Then I hand it back to him.

Sean glances at the paper and then looks up at me. "Are you coming on to me, Miss Smith?"

"Don't be absurd." I'm so sleepy that I can't tell if I'm thinking clearly. But it seems like a good idea, so I go with it. "It's a business contract, nothing more, nothing less. I heard you're a business man."

"I am, which is why there needs to be an additional clause..." Sean takes the paper and adds something.

When he hands it back to me, my stomach flips. "Those aren't the usual terms."

Sean smirks at me. "I'm an unusual man. Besides, fucking a married woman once in a while would be hot. And in the meantime, you have your best friend close by."

My heart pounds harder. I didn't come here expecting this, but I'm not backing down. I snatch the pen and add a few terms and then push it back at him. "Oh," tapping the pen to my lips, I add, "and my fee is doubled since your terms are so specific." I don't expect him to go for it. I think I'm just calling his bluff—because marrying Trystan Scott is insane.

"And let me guess, you're cutting Black out of the deal?" Sean watches me with those blue eyes, slowly sliding them up and down my body as I write.

I don't look up. "Maybe."

"She'll come after you if she finds out."

"Is that a threat, Mr. Jones?" I step toward him and raise a brow, holding the paper in one hand.

"It is. If you don't follow through with your end, Black will find out and you won't like what happens next." The threat doesn't feel hollow, but the smile on his face negates his menace. Sean's hand strokes the edge of my cheek and dips down my neck, lingering above my chest.

We're back at the beginning, and it kills me.

I thought we'd come so far, but I'm back to signing contracts and agreeing to be his sex toy. That's exactly what the terms stipulate—I belong to him and agree to do what he says—including being Trystan's girlfriend and maybe more.

Softly, I ask, "Trystan knows?"

Sean nods, and moves around behind me. Whispering in my ear, he says, "Sign it." His hands are wrapped around my middle and his warm breath makes me want to melt into him. I want so many things in this moment, but the one that screams the loudest is that I wish he was real, I wish this was real.

I'm caught in the middle with no way out, and unsure as to whether or not Sean means to harm me, so I take the pen and scrawl my signature across the page. I don't think he'd hurt me, but after everything that's happened, who the hell knows? I can't chance it. Even exhausted, I have to keep playing along and trying to see where this road ends.

Sean snatches the paper away, and then tugs me to him. "Your payment, Miss Smith." He takes large bills from his wallet and tucks them in my waistband. "The contract is complete."

My stomach has fallen into my shoes. I can't believe we're back at the beginning again. It's like the first night I worked for Black and walked over to his table. When he realized I was the call girl, he was furious. He thought he'd been played by someone he trusted. That must be what I'm feeling now. Swallowing hard I ask, "So, now what?"

"Now, I give you something that I know will make you smile." Sean turns to his desk and pulls out a small present. "Open it."

"You bought me a present?" I stare at it, not bothering to hide the disbelief on my face. This is weird. I don't know what to make of him.

It's as if Sean can read my mind, because he says, "Just open it. Remember, you belong to me. Do as I say and don't ask questions." Sean folds his arms over his chest and leans in closer, obviously excited.

As I rip the paper, I mutter, "If this is a dog collar, we're going to have a serious conversation—oh my God." It's a dark frame and under the sheet of glass is a diploma with the name AVERY ANNA STANZ, complete with signatures and an embossed stamp.

I stare at it in disbelief. All the air has been stripped from my lungs and I can't breathe. I sacrificed everything for this and it still slipped between my fingers. I can't even manage a full sentence. "How? I never finished my finals. How did you get this? Is it even real?"

Sean laughs. "Yes, it's real. You worked your ass off for that. I told the Dean that your roommate died and that it was your final semester. He said that there was a bereavement policy that would allow you to pass your classes, which in turn earned you the degree. Someone just had to file the paperwork."

"You filed the paperwork?" He nods. Suddenly I feel sick. I worked my butt off for this and it's tainted with blood. My mouth is hanging open, staring in shock. "So, this is because Amber died? I get to graduate and her family gets nothing. Sean, this is wrong, I can't accept this—"

He takes my hands gently, as if he knows I'm about to lose it. I've been held together by a thread for so long and it's beyond frayed. "Avery, you earned this. If Amber and her boyfriend lived—if no one was hunting you like a fucking animal—then you would have gone to class. You would have gotten higher grades than the university gave you." He reaches for my shoulder, lifting a strand of hair, letting it slip between his fingers. "There's a reason they have that rule in place, and it's for people like you. You worked so hard and have come so far, despite everything that was thrown your way. Most people would have quit. You didn't."

My voice is too high, but I can't help it. "I can't take this. I didn't earn it. They died, Sean. Because of me." A tear escapes from my eye and rolls down my cheek. It splatters on the glass, obscuring my name. "I don't deserve this."

Sean wipes away another tear before it can drop. His warm hands cradle my face, but he doesn't force me to look up. Instead, I stare at the diploma while a whirlwind of feelings cyclone together inside my chest.

My parents were supposed to be here. They would have been proud. I had plans for graduate school and plans for life, now none of them will happen. At least that's what I thought. Getting the diploma changes things, but when I look at it, I don't see my struggles or my accomplishments—I see blood on an eyelet bedspread and the blank look on Amber's lifeless body.

At some point I start prattling these things, bearing my soul to Sean in a way I've not done in a long time. I wipe away a tear. "How am I supposed to be proud of this when every time I look at it the only thing I see is death?" I laugh nervously and avoid his gaze. "Now isn't a good time to return me, or throw back any of the dumbass things I've done lately. Don't push me Sean, I can't handle it."

Sean shifts his stance. He's been listening to me, closed off, with his arms plastered to his chest. However, with my last statement, his arms drop to his sides and he steps forward, closer. "I'm sorry things didn't happen the way you wanted. I'm sorry you feel like their blood is on your hands, but it's not. I also know that I can tell you that for twenty years and you won't hear it, so hear this—I never, ever thought I'd be this close to you again."

He suddenly falls silent, so I glance up. His eyes are on the carpet and his hands are in his hair, as if he doesn't know what to say. "I pushed you away, too hard, too many times. You deserve better."

We stare at each other for a moment. Neither of us speaks. Time stills and this feels like one of those points that matter. I can blow him off and we can go back to the squabbling or I can do something else, something different and see where it leads.

My face scrunches up as I try not to cry. Stepping forward, I put the diploma down and step into Sean's space and press my body to his chest, hoping his arms will come up around me. He's not good at comforting, and this embrace reminds him of Amanda, I know it does, so I've avoided it—but not anymore.

Slowly his hands lift and find my back. He slides them into place and holds onto me.

I go on, bearing my soul. "Naked Guy was a douchebag, but I wouldn't have wished that on him. He tried to hurt me, plus he launched those videos of me sexting all over. But Amber—she didn't deserve it. If every bitch in the world was shot, there'd be less than a dozen women remaining and a lot of horny men."

Sean stifles a giggle and nearly chokes, but he seems to sense what I'm thinking. "Listen to me, Avery. Amber was a cop, and she knew the risk going in. Her death isn't on your shoulders, and you shouldn't feel badly about getting your degree either. You worked for it. You sacrificed everything, every moral, every virtue, so you could have this degree."

I feel so conflicted. My past and my present have collided together. "I know, but now that I have it, it wasn't worth it. If I could go back and undo everything, I would."

"Everything?" His voice is light, nervous. He knows I'll tell him the truth.

Once I met Sean Ferro, my life became an untamed mess. I dropped the reigns the night he kissed me. Everything has run wild since then. I never thought I'd be standing here inside the Ferro mansion, next to this man, and yet here I am.

Pulling back, I look up at him. "Let's not be coy anymore. If you have a question, ask it."

"You know what I'm asking." He stiffens, and the line between his brows deepens with worry.

"That's like saying, *you know I love you.*" I say the last part in a dumb guy voice.

Sean smirks. "I don't sound like that."

"Then, ask me, Mr. Jones and I'll tell you the truth. What is it that you really want to know?"

Sean has a lump in his throat that he can't swallow. It feels like I'm torturing him, but if we're wading into new waters here, we're going together. I take his hand and try to catch his eye.

His voice comes out so soft, so insecure, that it nearly tears me in two. "Do you wish we never met?"

Chapter 4

His question, God, it's awful. I don't think, I don't judge, I just talk. I hope that letting the floodgates open will finally help me see where I need to go. "After my parents died, I lost everything—my family, my childhood home—everything. The night I jumped on the back of your bike was one of the worst nights I'd had since the cops came and told me that my parents were gone. All my earthly possessions were in that car, and that car—" I let out a rush of air and push my hair out of my face, "—was the only thing I had left of my dad. No one helped me. No one cared enough to do a damn thing. But you did. The guy you try so hard to hide from the rest of the world was out in full force that night. I wouldn't wish that away, not for anything."

Sean turns quickly, making it so I can't see his eyes. "Let me run a bath for you."

That was an unexpected response. Not the typical Sean reply. I step in front of him, and place my hand on his chest. There's a sheen on his eyes and I know he's choked up. I don't know what else to say and I want to see him smile. Looking up into his eyes I whisper, "There's no mention of baths in that contract."

"There's no point stipulating that we had to sell our souls and yet here we are. Somehow we both went down the same road." He looks down at me with a soft expression on his face. It's as if he wants to tell me something but doesn't know how to put it into words. Sean places his hand on my cheek and runs it down my face, feeling the smoothness of my skin.

I hesitate, and look up at him. I wonder where this softness is coming from and how long it will last. There have been too many times when a side of Sean has come out, only to be driven back into the darkness faster than I can blink. I try to remember that that's who he is. He's a man that darts in and out of the shadows. Sean Ferro wants to be unseen, unheard, and unknown. The problem is that he's stolen my heart, and every time he recedes into the shadows, it goes with him.

Clearing my throat, I ask, "What about you? Do you wish you'd driven on, and ignored me like everyone else?" It's a question that I always wanted to ask, but never have. That night changed both our lives. He could've driven on, he could've ignored me. If he had, things would've been so much simpler for him. Stopping could've been one of the biggest mistakes of his life.

Sean leans in close and presses his lips to my cheek, and then slowly moves to the other side of my face, repeating the motion. The touch is so tender, I want to cry. I steel myself for whatever is coming next, for whatever words come out of his mouth.

Sean's lips part and his crystal blue gaze locks with mine. The corners of his mouth lift and he says, "A woman that determined to get back something of questionable value—on her own—is a force to be reckoned with. There's no way I was passing you by."

He smiles as he says it, as if it were a secret that no one knew. He runs his hands over my face again, cupping my cheek, and sweeping his thumb over my skin. I think he's going to stop, I don't expect him to reveal more, he never does. But this time

Sean surprises me. He continues in this surreal confession of the night we met.

Continuing, he says, "You amazed me, which is something rare. I wanted to know everything about you as soon as I saw you sprint down the road. You're a fighter, brave and beautiful, and there is nothing I would have changed about that day. In fact, I thank God for it every time I close my eyes. You've changed my nightmares to dreams, taming my fears with your boldness. You've made yourself vulnerable for me, to me—trusted me when you had no reason to—and it's not quite what I want, we're not there yet, and it's my fault."

Before I can ask him what he means, Sean leans in slowly, leaving the slightest separation between us. The warmth of his lips slip over my mouth and I want to lean in and kiss him. Sean continues, "I'm vulnerable now. They all know, every single one of them, except you."

"Are you going to make me ask a question in my dumb guy voice?" I smile softly.

Sean laughs and shakes his head. His dark hair falls into his eyes. "I love you. I won't hide it anymore. Being apart from you is killing me. The secrets between us, the fact that you ran to my mother instead of me isn't right. I want you. I want your trust, and your love. I want to be the one who protects you and I want you to trust me in every sense of the word. You're my weakness, my addiction, and I'm not willing to give you up." He grins at me for a moment. "And obviously we'll need to make amendments to that contract, although I thought bathing was assumed, dirty girl." He presses his finger to my nose, copying my prior booping.

The corners of my lips tug up, suddenly feeling playful. "Ass."

"Beautiful." He says it with that sexy smirk.

"Deviant."

"Goddess," he breathes this as if I am life itself, as if he believes it's true.

The sincerity of his words, the intensity of them, throws me off balance. I laugh and shove his chest. "Jerkface."

Sean chortles and grabs my hands gently. "Get in the tub and I'll explain why you're marrying another man."

Chapter 5

I make a face showing just how much I detest this idea. "You were serious about that?"

"Why do you keep asking me that? When do I joke about anything?" Sean's voice is flat and serious.

"Touché."

Sean jokes about very little. The times that I can get him to lighten up and I can see those darling dimples, and hear that hypnotic laugh—I live for those times. I guess that means he seriously wants me to marry Trystan Scott. I can't imagine Trystan would agree to it, so I don't freak out then and there. Besides, Sean can't tell me who to marry.

I glance around the room and see the framed paper again. The center of my chest tugs. Looking at the framed diploma, reading my name in the center of the document, it's just too much. Sean sees me glancing at it.

Gesturing, I say, "Thanks for this."

It's too little to say, I know that. But how do you thank someone for something like this? I would've gone on the rest of my life with no diploma, not knowing that I'd earned it or that I could even get it.

There are people that watch out for you, there are people that watch *over* you, and until this moment I thought they were gone. The night my parents died, I lost all that. I had no one watching out for me, no one watching over me.

Sometimes it seems like Sean wants to be that guy, while other times it seems like he wants to be a Ferro. I wish Sean would drop his guard long enough for me to see who he really is, long enough for *him* to see who he really is, because I don't think he knows. I don't think Sean sees the man that he's become. He still thinks he's the monster, the man that was scorned and mocked and ridiculed, the demon trapped in this godforsaken place. And I came along sprinting down Deer Park Avenue chasing my crap car, and his world changed.

Our worlds collided that night.

Sean turns his sapphire gaze my way. He says it like it's nothing and everything at the same time. "You sold your soul for that diploma. I know how much it meant to you. It was the least I could do." Sean reaches for the hem of his shirt and slips it over his head, tossing it onto his bed, before turning and offering me his hand.

I'm beyond shocked at the turn of events. I want to drop my guard but every time I've done it in the past, I got sucker-punched in the face. There are only so many more hits I can take before I become permanently ugly, inside and out.

I step toward him, uncertain. "And this bath of yours, is it part of the Barbie Dream House or are we going to fill a big ass box with water?"

Sean laughs out loud and grabs my wrist. Pulling me against his bare chest, he's all smiles. "You shouldn't have come."

"You keep saying that." I smile. It feels like I'm going to explode inside. When he first said those words I thought they were a warning that I should leave. I thought I was in danger, but I'm not—Sean is the one who is in danger as long as I'm around.

Sean answers, "Because it means you're never going to get rid of me, and the crazy ass future you'll have because of it. I'm worried and elated. It feels like I'm bursting with joy and being ripped apart with guilt. I should have rolled you out of the mansion, onto the doormat, and kicked the door shut."

My eyes bug out. "That would have been pretty nasty, Sean Ferro. Rich people have some pretty crappy manners. It's deplorable. What would your mother think?"

He smirks. "My mother taught me how to survive, and I'm going to teach you the same thing. But instead of being three steps ahead of you and leaving you in the dark, I'll take you with me. Every step. Every second."

Oh my God, he's serious. Is this it? This is the moment I've been waiting for?

His jaw isn't locked and his touch is light. I can see the conflict burning in his eyes, but he's already decided.

I don't know if I should die or dance. I'm still leery though, so much has happened. I still don't trust him, not fully. The problem is that I want to. Coyly, I ask, "So what's three steps from now?"

A wicked smile spreads across his lips. "You, naked, tied to the Tantra chair."

"Dibs."

"Dibs?" A curious expression slips across his face. "What is this, middle school? What are you calling dibs on?"

Grinning widely, I walk toward him. "Apparently our plans for the evening are going in the same direction, but on step three I planned on having you tied up on that chair. Dibs." I move my mouth slowly, letting my lips hug the word. "I call dibs on the sex chair."

Sean offers a crooked smirk and takes my hand, pulling me ahead, into another room. "Spray Start Car Girl, I knew you'd be awesome." I follow him, laughing.

Chapter 6

I'm about to make some witty comeback when every word in my head is suddenly gone. "Holy shit!" We enter a side room, and from how dark it was inside I thought it was a pass-through or a closet, but it's not. It's Sean's shower, bath, and bat cave all in one. The walls are black glass tile with accents of dark blue here and there. Black marble basins sit in front of an ornate antique mirror that has Tiffany lamps fixed to the mirrors.

Pointing, I jabber, "Are those real?"

Sean laughs. "Never ask a man if it's real."

"Uh, you're never supposed to ask a girl if they are real."

Sean smirks and then says, "Everything in here is real."

"So you put multimillion dollar lamps in your bathroom. Okay." I shrug like that's normal. He has rubies in his book case, so what the hell do I know?

Sean ignores my snark and takes my wrist, pulling me around a curved wall. As soon as I see it, I gasp. A copper soaking tub sits alone in front of a wall, which is covered in tiny tiles of blue, gold, and purple. Water trickles down the tiles from a decorative scupper, flowing all the way down behind the tub. Gold and silver handles sit on a pedestal with a sprayer. On the side walls there are two iron sconces that are at least six feet tall, complete with candles and flickering flames.

Eyes wide, I gasp, "Oh my God. It's girl porn!"

Sean laughs as I ditch him to run over and look at the tub more carefully. His deep voice booms behind me. "So, at least I know where I stand in the scheme of things." He folds his arms over his toned chest.

Touching the cool copper tub, I look back at him. "Why do you have this? It's as if you planned on using it every night of your life… because let's face it, twenty year old Sean wasn't into mind fucks and boxes. Was he?" I glance around, looking for a stack of crates.

Sean smirks, revealing that lickable dimple, and takes my face in his hands. "I made this thinking that I'd want to share it with someone special one day. I was the heir, this house would have been mine, so my suites were all over the top lavish." Sean tips his head to the side, watching my reaction, drinking in my movements.

"Did you ever use it?" I'm tracing my fingers along the edge of the tub and staring at the waterwall, too afraid to look at him. I'm sure he used it. He had to use it.

"Yes, frequently."

My stomach sinks and I turn slowly to look at him. He's trying not to smile. I stand and walk over to him as the corner of my mouth tugs up and my stomach sinks. "So, were these bathing interludes solo?" Stupid question, but one can hope.

His smile stretches further. "Perhaps." He looks down at me with those solid arms still pressed against his body.

My gaze flicks between his muscles and his eyes. "What's it going to take to get details?"

"Tit for tat, Stanz. Tell me about your previous lovers and I'll tell you about mine." Sean leans against the wall and unfolds his arms revealing his sculpted bare chest. He seems amused, like this idea could be fun.

Blinking repetitively, I blurt out, "You just wanted to say *tit*." I wink at him and then stand up and walk over to the waterwall, looking at each piece of cut glass. "Besides, I told you, you're my first."

Sean shakes his head. "But I wasn't your only. I caught that one night when you were ranting. There was a rich guy and...?" His voice trails off, waiting for me to answer and fill in all the things that I don't really want to say.

I glance back at Sean and decide to just tell him. "And that guy liked my tits, too. His family thought I was a gold digger and broke us up on the night of our prom." I say it stoically, even though it still burns.

"They didn't bother to tell me though, so I got dressed and waited. He never came. Well, he probably did come, but it wasn't with me. We had plans to spend the weekend together at his family's summer home out east. They had a house in South Hampton. After that whole episode I turned into a lesbian and swore off men forever." I smile over my shoulder. Sean's lips are parted like he believes the last part. I pick up a bar of soap and chuck it at him. It hits his shoulder and falls to the floor.

He blinks and grins. "Sorry, tits and lesbian in the same conversation. I knew it was too good to be true."

I laugh. "You were mentally ordering bigger boxes for a three-way. Admit it."

Sean shakes his head and steps toward me. "No three-ways. Ever. Not my thing. No women in this tub. The truth is that Amanda didn't like being in the mansion. She thought my mother had cameras everywhere."

"She probably does. Connie's a creeper." I glance around, looking for little black orbs with hidden cameras.

"There aren't any, not unless I installed them." Sean smiles wickedly and tugs at my shirt. "This is in the way."

I stop him from taking it off. "No, no. Wait a second. This was the ex-lover talk. I had one, that I never actually had sex with, and then didn't date again. The humiliation from something like that doesn't disappear in a day or two. Then I had to watch out for myself and getting knocked up wasn't something that I could deal with. That explains my incredibly low dating record. But you, there were others besides Amanda. Who was your first?" This is a question I've been dying to ask. Sean's face flushes which shocks me. "Oh God, you're blushing. Please tell me that you didn't nail your cousin?"

Sean's jaw drops, shocked. "No! Why would you even say that? Do you see this?" He points to his perfectly defined abs and smooth skin. "I had to turn down women all the time." He reaches past me and turns on the water, letting the tub fill. When he straightens, he wraps his arms around my waist and tugs me to him. "My first was in high school."

"Uber private prep boy nails socialite's daughter to the wall?"

Sean runs a hand through his hair, pushing it out of his eyes. "Something like that. Anyway, I knew guys had conquests—they'd talk about getting into some girl's panties, nail her, and then choose a new target. I was a little naïve and didn't realize that women did it, too." He's still smiling, but it's sad, like he wishes the story were different.

"Oh my God. She notched you on her belt and walked away?"

He corrects, "She made love to me and walked away, then quickly told all of her friends at school all the details, like how big it is, how long I lasted, lots of things about length, size, and stamina. All things that a high school boy might find horrifying."

I laugh a little because it's terrible. "So that's why you fuck? No lovemaking?"

"Fucking is intense, but I can keep my guard up."

Okay, affirmative then. "What about your wife? Did you let her in, or should I not ask things like that?" Crap. I shouldn't have asked. I feel horrible, but his lips part as he starts to answer me. I am too shocked to stop him.

His face becomes pale and those dark lashes lower. "If I did lower my guard, it wasn't often. That's why I couldn't tell. That's why—"

Stepping forward, I press my finger to his lips. "I shouldn't have asked."

He takes my hand and kisses the back gently, closing his eyes and feeling my skin against his cheek. "We both have ghosts, past lives. They'll come out periodically. They can present themselves as shadows or banshees. If we know about each other, we'll be better prepared to deal with them."

"I agree. Just don't promise to take me to prom and then not show up." I smile at him and pull Sean into my arms. "And for the record, I like fucking you. Making love sounds weird."

He pulls away and shakes his head. He arches a brow at me. "You're not getting out of it, Miss Smith. Anything and everything is mine and I'm not in a fucking kind of mood right now. Maybe later, but not now."

My lips part as my skin covers in goose bumps, and I take a step back. My heel hits the edge of the tub and I stumble. Sean catches me just as I fall into the water, which pulls him in and makes him land on top of me.

I start laughing. The waterwall is pouring over my hair and twigs are floating in the tub. Sean starts laughing with me. "This should be a picture on the urban dictionary page for 'smooth move.' I have half a forest in my frickin' hair! Why didn't you say anything?"

Sean kicks his shoes off and they splatter next to the tub. He plucks a stick from the water and smiles. "You looked adorable, like a little forest elf that got bitch-slapped by a tree."

I shove his chest and splash some of the tub water at him. Sean's laughter is light like mine, and it's nice to hear him in such a good mood. The tone is so rich and carefree, so unburdened from the things that I usually hear from him.

The tub is big enough for both of us to stand, and so we do, splashing each other like children. Water goes flying everywhere, hitting Sean in the face and soaking his jeans. Eventually, he steps towards me and wraps me in his arms. His mouth comes down on mine, slowly, warm and welcome. The embrace is so tender for him, so unlike him, that I wonder what he's going to do next.

Chapter 7

I'm used to the way Sean moves, fast and hard, the way he controls me. This time though, that's not the man that's with me. Instead, I have a different version of Sean. He's slow and seeking, tracing the lines of my mouth with his tongue while cupping my cheeks with his hands. He turns me so that the waterfall is over both of us, warming us. The movements he makes aren't controlling. They're vulnerable and sweet.

I reach for his buckle, pulling the wet leather through the belt loops of his jeans. I toss it aside. There's water everywhere, but he doesn't care. Sean's gaze fixes on me, watching me, wondering what I'm going to do next. Reaching out for his hands, I take them and put them on the hem of my shirt, inviting him to finish what he started. Sean takes the damp fabric in his hands and slowly slides it up over my head and tosses it to the floor.

Those sky-blue eyes wander over my slick curves before returning to my face. I expect him to go for my bra and throw it off, guessing that he'll be harsh and forceful, the way he usually is—but not this time.

Instead, Sean takes the tip of his finger, and barely touching my skin, chases the water as it flows down from my neck to my shoulder and finally to my breast. The pads of his fingers barely touch my skin. The effect is a symphony of sensations. I gasp and look up at him. Sean pushes my wet hair out of my face, and cups my chin, holding my gaze on his.

"You really should not have come." This time when Sean says the words, I hear the real meaning and it scares me to death.

Chapter 8

The intensity of Sean's gaze makes me shiver. He mistakes the motion as coldness and steps out of the tub to grab a towel. He returns quickly and wraps it around me. "Come here for a few minutes, let me run you the type of bath that I was planning on giving you."

My stomach swirls as Sean takes my hand and helps me step over the side of the tub. He sits me down on a cedar bench next to the shower. Sean hands me a fluffy white towel that I wrap around my body.

Now I'm shivering because I'm cold. Before Sean goes back to clean up the mess he does something unexpected. Reaching up under the towel, he finds my waistline and gently removes my pants and my panties. He doesn't look at them, he doesn't put my intimates to his nose and inhale. Instead, he just takes the damp clothing and puts it down a laundry chute. Before he walks away he gives me a kiss on the cheek and smiles. "I'll warm you up fast. Just give me a minute."

"Sean?" I'm not sure what he's doing or what he wants from me. The way he's acting is unnerving.

He was walking away, but when I call his name he stops and turns. I don't know what to say, so I sit there with my mouth hanging open. I can tell him the truth, I can tell him that I'm scared, that this is too close to what I want—to what I've always wanted—and that if he's pretending now, it'll kill me. The words never come to my mouth but they must be in my eyes, because he seems to know.

"I won't hurt you, Avery. Not again. I know you have no reason to trust me, and I know too much has happened between us, but I promise you, this is me. The guy they kept thinking wasn't there, the one that I denied, but this is who I am." He shrugs like it's nothing, but at that moment I can tell he is as afraid as I am.

Pressing my lips together, I say, "Well, just so you know, you are nothing to shrug at. And I understand why you kept him hidden. We both needed two things to survive, things that were unbecoming."

Sean doesn't know how to respond— there's a look of relief on his face and a half smile. It molds his lips into an adorable expression. I want to jump up and kiss him. It's scary, but I think I'm finally getting to see the side of Sean that I know is there, revealed to me full force. Sean's finally stopped hiding who he is, at least in front of me. The monsters have been left in the shadows and I finally have him, all of him.

I don't know if I should hold back or give in. This chance may not come again, and I don't want to regret holding back. At the same time my heart's so brittle, so marred, that I'm afraid to open it up entirely again. I could manage fucking, I was so sure that I made a freaking contract. I didn't think to exclude this part. I didn't think Sean would try to make love to me and now that he has, I don't know what to do.

Some people say be careful what you wish for. I used to think that was because wishes don't come true. That's not what I'm seeing in front of me now. This version of Sean's raw and real, ready to give me everything I've always wanted. The question is, am I? Or will I be a frightened little girl and run away?

I told him to stop beating around the bush. Well, that has a whole other meaning that I never thought of. Damn. Maybe it's time for me to be brave, to step out of the shadows myself. This is my chance to get what I've always wanted, even if it's only once.

Besides, he's already broken me so many times I don't see how I could be worse off than before. He sees my eyes and, in that moment, I swear to God he knows what I'm thinking.

"Avery, this is for you. I dropped my walls for you and only you. And you can say no. I'm not pressuring you into this. I know you've been hurt by me, by life. I wouldn't blame you." His voice trails off at the end of the sentence, like he would be in agony if I said no.

The truth falls from my lips before I can stop it, "I'm afraid."

"So am I." Sean watches me from across the room as he refills the tub preparing it with oils and lighting candles that float on the surface of the water. For a moment neither of us breathe, we just stare at each other silently. He offers an uncertain smile before he turns back to the water, adjusting the temperature, picking up twigs that fell from my hair.

When he finishes, he walks over to the shower where I'm sitting. There are over six shower heads and a control panel that I have no clue how to use. He presses three or four buttons and all of a sudden there's wonderful warm steam and a trickle of hot water from overhead.

Sean extends his hand. "You can rinse off before you bathe. There's soap and shampoo to get the wilderness off of you. We can check your cuts when you come out. Oh, and there's a pink bottle, on the far right, that's for you."

That last statement caught my attention. What on in the world could he have gotten me? I drop the fuzzy warm towel and head into the steam, inhaling deeply as I go.

Oh. My. God. It feels so good. It's a shower that feels as though it's raining inside. The water falls gently, pouring over my body. I look around for the pink bottle and see it right away. It's made of crystal and has a jeweled topper. I remove the lid and bring my head to the opening of the bottle, inhaling deeply. It smells incredible. I can't decide what it's made from. The scents are familiar, but I can't place them.

I pour some of it into my hand, unsure as to whether it's perfume or soap. When I put the bottle down and start rubbing, it's clear from the lather that it's soap. I rub it on my arms and my stomach and my legs, removing the remains of running through the woods, and tripping over fences. My muscles go slack in the heat and I can feel sleep catching up with me.

That's when Sean comes to fetch me. He has a white fluffy towel wrapped around his waist and nothing else. His hair is damp as if he showered somewhere else. He takes my hand, presses a button on the way out so the shower turns off, and leads me back to the waterfall next to the bathtub.

Holding onto his arm, I feel weary. "I am so tired."

Sean runs his fingers through my damp hair and down my neck, bracing my shoulders. "I know, but this can't wait any longer. I think it's something we both wanted for a long time, isn't it?"

Looking up into his eyes, all I can do is nod. Gently, he takes my hand and leads me over to the copper tub. Sean helps me in and tells me to lean back. I do as he says, and close my eyes. The sound of the water wall is perfect, combined with the candles and gentle scents—it's perfection.

Sean asks me to lean back and lifts my hair over the side of the tub. I try to turn to see what he's doing but he tells me to relax. "I told you," he says. "This is something I have wanted to do for a while. If you don't like it let me know, but I think you will."

My nerves are jumbled because I can't begin to fathom what he's going to do. Is he going to pull my hair? Is he going to cut it? Just as the next thought enters my mind, I feel what he's doing. The same scent from the pink bottle that was in the shower stall, I smell it, and I know he's lathering it into my hair. I feel the cool liquid pool on the top of my head before Sean's fingers work it into my scalp. He massages my temples, gently and carefully untangling my hair with his fingers as he works that wonderful smell into it.

Sean's voice is timid, which is so unlike him. "I had this made for you a while back. I didn't know how to give it to you. I never thought you'd come here, not with me."

I try not to moan as he rubs my head, "I can't place the scents. What are they?"

As Sean pours warm water over my hair, rinsing the soap, he answers, "They're things that remind me of you, that I kind of jumbled together. The scent of the ocean and newly fallen snow. The crispness of the winter air, and the smell of a fire. I basically asked them to make it smell like bottled snowman, but for a chick." He laughs and continues, "Peter's cologne guy in Italy nearly died when I asked him to do it. The funny part is, he said of course he could do anything, but when I told him what I wanted him to create, he just blinked at me."

I'm spacing out on him, almost falling asleep, but I think I heard Peter and perfume in the same sentence. I sit up in the tub and turn to look at him, "You made this for me?"

Sean nods. "It's the things that remind me of you. The only thing I didn't add was ether."

I laugh at that. "Thank God. I've spent enough of my life smelling like a nasty car. I can't believe you did this. How long ago did you—"

"Too long ago. I didn't know what to do, Avery. Sorry it took me so long."

"Me too, because I'm pretty sure I'm gonna fall asleep."

"Oh, I assure you that you will be awake and delighted, squealing like a schoolgirl."

A smile twists my lips and I look back at him, wondering what sparked this change and how long he'll stay like this. I know Sean said he won't go back again, that he won't revert, but he's said that before. At the same time, he's never done anything like this before, ever.

I tip my head back to make some witty remark but before I do, Sean's lips are on mine pressing a gentle kiss. I moan inwardly, thinking how much I'm going to like this.

Chapter 9

I follow Sean's sexy, naked butt into the shower where he takes my face between his hands and leans in slowly. The kiss is different this time. There's no hurried desperation, but the kisses are still hungry and passionate. As we melt into one another, Sean uses his body to push me against the wall.

The conflicting coolness of the tile and the heat from the shower peak my senses. I gasp and let out a rush of air as Sean's lips travel down my neck and onto my shoulder. He stays there, teasing me, kissing that spot that makes me so weak. My fingers tangle in his hair, holding on tightly and not wanting us to stop. My fatigue washes away and is replaced with something else, something that's warm and wanted.

It's hard for me to stand there and not move. Sean's warm mouth presses firmly against my skin, trailing down my neck, and onto my shoulder. His teeth graze my skin, nipping as his tongue flicks against me. His hands are on my sides. They slowly slip around to my butt and he cups my ass and holds on tight. He presses his hard length against me, teasing me, as he does so. Water is pouring over my face and drizzling down my breasts. There are so many sensations.

My stomach pools with warmth and spreads within me. Holding him is not enough, tugging his hair isn't getting him where I want him to go. So I beg softly, "Please?"

And with a husky voice he replies, "Not yet. I want to kiss you first. I want to make you feel so incredibly sexy, and I want you to scream out my name at the top of your lungs. 'Please' does not suffice." His lips immediately lower as he trails down toward my breasts.

He leans in close, slowly, putting his lips on my body. I gasp with excitement, holding onto his hair, encouraging him. His mouth traces over my curves, wrapping around my breast, slowly and painfully making his way toward my nipple. The way he does it is so erotic and so sensual that my hips start to grind against his. But Sean won't allow it, he uses his hands to hold me still.

I moan his name and try to wriggle against him, but he just presses me tighter to the wall. Water cascades over us, making our skin slick. The friction feels different and wonderful. Moaning, I tangle one hand in his hair while the other reaches for him. Before I can touch, he grabs my hand and pins it to the wall.

"I'm surprised you didn't have handcuffs built into the shower." I tease him, but my voice catches when he sucks my nipple into his mouth.

He plays with the taut peak, flicks his tongue across the top and nips me with his teeth. The response is instant and my hips buck against him once more. Before I can wiggle into the right spot, his hand comes down on my butt, slapping me gently. The water makes the sting and the sound more intense even though his touch was light.

My breath catches in my throat when Sean looks up at me. His eyes are midnight blue and those lashes are so dark. His hair is dripping, hanging in his eyes as he watches me. "I want you so much. You have no idea."

I wiggle my hips against him and smirk. "I think I may have a little bit of an idea."

Sean offers a lopsided smile. "Never call it little."

"No, little Sean?"

I think he's going to answer, but he doesn't. Instead, he grabs the bottle of soap he had made for me and opens the stopper. He pulls me forward, out of the stream of water, before tipping the bottle on its side. The pink colored soap drips out and lands on my chest. Sean eyes me with a wicked smirk as he does it, drizzling the entire contents of the bottle on my chest, across my breasts, and on my stomach. When he finishes, he sets the jar down on the shelf behind me. Then he presses his body to mine.

"Oh God." I gasp, as the suds make our bodies slicker.

Sean rubs his chest to mine, moving up and down against me, making every inch of me slick. Sean stops after a few moments and grabs a padded mat. He tosses it on the floor. "Kneel."

I don't ask what he wants, I just do it, expecting that my reward will be that hard length of his in my mouth. It makes me wetter just thinking about Sean pulling my hair as he buries himself in my mouth. As he stands in front of me, he takes that gorgeously hard part of him and touches it to my cheek. I lift my hands to take hold and pull him into my mouth, but Sean scolds me.

"No. Hands down until I say so."

I nod, dropping my hands to my sides once more. I bite my bottom lip as my gaze fixates on him. It's right in front of me and I really, really want it now. I want to savor his warmth and the way he tastes. But that's not what Sean has in mind, because he steps closer to me again, and caresses my face with his hardness. He starts on one cheek and slowly pulls it across, passing over my closed lips quickly, and then slowing as he reaches the other side of my face. He repeats the movement, watching me tremble.

"Please let me suck you," I moan the words, watching him and wanting him to let me.

"Not yet."

I moan again, but stop quickly because he uses that second to brush the tip across the seam of my lips. I open for him and he pushes inside quickly. I only get to wrap my tongue around him for a moment before he pulls out. We both moan loudly, and gasp for air.

The room continues to fill with steam as water pours down Sean's back. His breathing is heavy and rapid, like mine. When he leans in toward my mouth again, I part my lips, but that's not where he's going. Sean leans against the wall, which puts his dick about a foot lower—right in front of my girls. He holds them, pressing them together and then slips his firm length in between. His thumbs play with my nipples as he rocks his hips into my cleavage.

The familiar sensation is building within me. It feels like my veins are filled with lust and I have to have him now. I can't...oh god. It feels good. Before I know what happens, he's fucking my cleavage as I watch. My moans become high pitched, wanting more. The spot between my legs is begging for attention as it throbs, becoming wetter and wetter.

"Beg me, baby."

I can't help it. I want him so much that I have no pride at all. I plead with him, "I want you. Fuck me, please. Come on me, come in me. I need you, Sean. Baby, please. I want to taste you and suck you. Feed it to me?" I wiggle against him, making the boob fuck better. He groans and reaches out for the wall, as if he's unable to stand like that any longer.

"Where do you want me to come?"

A sexy grin spreads across my lips. "Like this. Do exactly what you're doing, and at the last second lift it to my lips and come in my mouth. I want to taste you so badly."

"I will, but only if you play too." I don't follow his meaning. "Put your fingers where I can't reach. Touch yourself and come with me." Our eyes are locked, and for a moment, everything feels perfect. I'm loved. This isn't fucking—it's scary and wonderful at the same time.

It's as if he can read my mind. "I love you, Avery. Please do that for me. I want to see your face when you shatter."

I answer by putting my hand at the V between my legs and press my fingers against that sensitive spot. As I start to rub, Sean takes my breasts and resumes slipping between them.

Sean groans with pleasure, which only makes my hand move faster. We're both on edge, ready to lose it. His hips are bucking into me and the frantic pace of his movements lets me know how close he is. My fingers rub against that spot between my legs and then slip inside. We're both moving together, thrusting and moaning, getting higher and higher.

I call out his name, and dig my nails into his ass. He gasps and thrusts a few more times, before pulling out from between my breasts. His hot, hard length goes straight between my lips. He straightens and grabs hold of my hair as he pushes into my mouth. Sean makes the sexiest sounds as my mouth fills with his sweet come. I suck, swallowing it, wanting to taste it forever. My fingers frantically move between my legs as he pushes in deeper, and I feel the hot liquid drip down my throat. My hips buck into my hand as he does it and I find my release. My hands lift as I hold onto him, guiding him to remain at my lips and to continue pumping into me. I hold the strong curve of his butt in my hands as I suck and swallow. My tongue slides along his shaft as he pulls out and pushes in. Sean cries out as he finishes and his grip on me loosens.

He immediately pulls away, mortified. "Oh my god. I'm so sorry."

On my knees, I look up at him. "There's nothing to be sorry for. I loved it."

Sean hesitates. "I've never fucked your face that hard before. Are you sure you're okay?"

Leaning in close, I press a kiss against the V in his legs, right in the perfect place. "I'm more than okay. I wanted it. I wanted you. I love you."

He takes my hands and lifts me, pulling me against his chest. "I love you too. I hope you feel like letting me show you how much."

I smile against his warm skin. "I'd like that."

Chapter 10

After the shower, Sean takes me to his bed, carrying me like a bride across the room. He loves me slowly and softly until we are both sated again. Then we lie tangled together, skin on skin, on top of Sean's posh bedding. It feels like raw silk beneath my fingers. Caressing the bedspread, I slide my hand over the surface, feeling the small bumps of the natural threads beneath my finger. We're both tired and exhausted, not able to move, but not willing to sleep. This day, this week, has been unimaginable. Add to it this night, and I would've never thought this could happen, not in a million years. I'm in Sean Ferro's bed in the Ferro mansion, being cradled in his arms.

Sean's breath is warm in my ear. He's been silent for a while now. The sun has set and night has fallen. His room is absolutely still. There's no noise from trains or cars or highways. It's just him and me, his breath in my breath.

I wonder if he's contemplating what we're going to do next or if he's sated and ready to sleep. It isn't until he talks that I know. Tucking a curl behind my ear, he whispers, "Why do you always come back to me?"

I can't help it, my lips tighten up. "Why do you always feel like you have to push me away?"

I feel Sean smile behind me, as his cheek presses to my neck. "You didn't answer my question, Miss Smith"

"Ditto, Mr. Jones." Shifting, I snuggle my back into his front, and Sean holds me tighter. "I'm thinking that these may be questions that we'll never have answers to. Am I supposed to stop asking? I feel like I should know, but I don't. This doesn't even feel real. This thing between us feels like love and it scares me to death. Sometimes I want to run, but being without you—I just can't do that. Maybe love is as fragile as a snowflake, but we both know I like the cold." The memory makes me smile. It brings me back to the day in the snow, sledding with Sean. That was like today, like right now. It's surreal because I thought I'd never see that man again. I'm still not sure if things will stay the same once we leave this bed, actually I'm terrified of it ending.

Sean runs his fingers over my curves, down my side and over my hip where he rests his hands "Yes, we know that for sure. We also know that no matter what I do, you come back. I don't know what I've done to deserve you, I feel like you must've done something horrible to deserve me—"

Turning back, I look at him. "Stop it. You keep saying things like that, you keep acting like you're beyond saving, but you are not. I know what's real and what's fake. I know you're afraid the same way I am, but is it better to be alone? I had thought so, but building up all these walls and becoming numb doesn't keep you from feeling. I still feel every bit of remorse, every pang of pain, and every bit of guilt. I thought walls would save me from that, I thought pushing people away and making myself numb was the only way I could endure, but I was wrong. Those walls, those barricades I built to keep people out—they worked. They kept people out, but they also locked me inside with all my agony. I know what that feels like, and I know you do too."

Sean presses his lips to my temple slowly and softly. His strong arms wrap around me, holding me tightly. My heart beats faster and faster as the moments pass. He says nothing. I don't know if I've guessed wrong, if only I feel that way and he doesn't, or if he's regretting this intimacy with me—but Sean's silence is unnerving. I could speak and break it, I could pass over it like the comments meant nothing, like they were meant in jest, but they weren't.

When I feel his lips part, I have no idea what he is going to say. "I don't like admitting this part but I made a mistake, Avery. Some mistakes can't be undone. I've been festering in anguish and blaming myself for Amanda, for losing everything that was important to me, for not being there for Peter, for bailing on Jon. I've lost them, Avery. And the thing is, I can't bear to lose you too. Whenever that thought surfaces I raise my guard and push you away. It's the only way I knew how to survive. No one's come back, except you. I've never broken a promise to my mother before. I know it seems like a strange thing to say in the middle of a conversation when the most beautiful woman in the world is lying naked next to me, but I swore you'd be gone and here you are."

"So, how are you going to get rid of me? Because the box thing didn't work." I smile and shiver at the same time. Sean notices and rubs my arms chasing the chill away.

"Well, I planned on arranging your marriage to someone I can't stand to make sure we didn't see too much of each other and to satisfy my mother, but the main reason I was doing it was to keep you safe." Sean's grip around my waist tightens. "Trystan's staff, his security team, is older than mine and less likely to have been tampered with by any of the Ferro's. Unlike our security team that's obviously been tampered with. That guy Bob, that mountain of a man that Trystan always has around, I know he can watch out for both of you in a way that I can't. It seemed to me that his lifestyle would suit you better and that you would be better protected. As it is, I'm having to go back through all the employees that we've had to see which ones were tainted, and speculate who ruined them. My pilot for example, no one should have been able to corrupt him, but someone did. You're safer with Trystan."

This part frightens me. He's serious when he says these things, when he thinks he can marry me off as if that would solve everything. "I'm not marrying Trystan. If there's a wedding, there's only one man I want to marry and he's behind me, holding me tight. Besides the man gunning for me is dead. You have the papers they want, so the power vacuum is gone. You won and we can be together. I'm not totally naïve Sean, I know what this means, what you are going to do. I've made decisions that I thought I would never make, and I did things that I thought I would never do, and all in the name of survival. If this is what you need to do to survive, I'm with you, and by your side."

I feel Sean move his jaw before he finally speaks. "You don't know what you're agreeing to, you don't know what you're offering. There are things that I can't say within these walls, but would make your blood run cold. I've come back covered in blood, I've done things that I can't confess, things that weigh heavily on my heart—things that have destroyed my soul. That's not the life I want for you, but that is my life, this is my life, and there's no way out." Sean kisses the back of my neck before he pushes away.

He swings his feet over the side of the mattress and stands up before walking over to one of the massive windows. He stands there for a moment and then pulls back the drapes. Sean stares through the glass at the moonlight and the tall cypress trees that line the front drive. The reflecting pools in the gardens outside make his face glow softly.

As I watch him, I wonder what he's done and why he thinks he can't be redeemed. I roll on my side and prop my head up with my hand, looking at him, I ask, "What if we did it together? What if we took over Campone's investments together? I can keep you from falling off the cliff and you can do the same for me. It would protect your brothers, and shove your mother out of the middle. I don't think we can take all of his endeavors," I smile, confessing that I don't know exactly what Campone was running, unless you consider bribery, drugs, prostitution and that sort of thing as properties in normal investments, "and make them into something good. I can't stand Miss Black, but if I hadn't found that job, I would've been homeless. I had no other options. Sean, prostitution is legal in some states, and there's a reason for it. It's one of the oldest businesses in the world, right?" Did I just say that? Sean turns slowly, dropping the draperies. I wink at him.

Sean presses his lips together forming a tight seam. His blue eyes drop to the carpet as he walks over to the bed and sits down on the side. His gaze lowers to my hand, which he lifts, taking it in his own, and presses it to his lips. "If only it were that simple. This is blood money, Avery. The entire company runs on fear and is fueled by blood. There is no good in it, there's only power. That's why my mother wants it so badly. If she can own everything that Campone had, then she will be unstoppable. Wealth, power, dirty secrets. In short, she'll own every wealthy family in New York. That legacy will be passed on to Jon, and I can't let that happen. I failed them once, I am not doing it again. That's why I need to get there first. I don't want Peter, Jon—or hell—even Hallie, dragged back here. The only way to make sure that doesn't happen is if I'm the point man."

"I understand what you're saying, and I'm saying you don't have to do it alone."

"This is a slippery slope, Avery. I can't let you step onto it."

I laugh at that. Leaning closely, I place a finger on his cheek, saying, "Don't give me the morality speech, not from you. Besides, I don't believe that crap. People can choose to be good and people can choose to be bad. Good people can do bad things and bad people can do good things. No one is intrinsically anything. Besides, from what you just said, you want to make sure you're the one with the power to save your brothers and the people they care about. That doesn't sound bad to me." I touch his shoulder, leaving my hand there, feeling the strong, firm muscles beneath my grip.

He is so tense and so worried about me. Sean glances at me out of the corner of his eye as if he's acknowledging that I'm right, albeit reluctantly. I give him a lopsided smile in return and say, "Love can make you do all sorts of crazy things. Some are earth shattering while others seem mundane. The thing is, you and I found each other, and a love like we have is rare, like fairytale territory."

"So does that make you Cinderella?" Sean smiles at me, revealing that dimple.

The comparison makes me laugh. "Are you saying Cinderella was a hooker? Because I know she got with the prince a little fast, but I thought it was because of the pumpkin coach. Unless that was like slang for some kind of STD. In which case she gave it to the Prince. And let's face it, Prince Charming was a wuss. He didn't do anything except bring a bunch of girls one shoe. Who the hell wants one shoe?" The thought makes me laugh, as the comparison becomes clear in my mind. "Holy shit, did you say your mom is like the evil stepmother?"

Sean starts laughing. It's way too late and we're way too tired, because I'm sure this wasn't a funny joke but for some reason it makes both of us laugh hysterically. "I don't think anybody would deny it."

"Then let's steal her happily ever after. Fuck everyone else. Break the glass slipper, I know you can. My Prince Charming has pumpkin-sized balls." I can barely get the words out without laughing, partly because it's true, and partly because it's a really good visualization for Sean Ferro. Apparently he thinks so too because he leans into me giggling—giggling. The man is *giggling*.

"That makes Jon and Pete the ugly stepsisters." That deep booming laugh comes from deep within him. It's a rare sound that I absolutely love to hear.

"So you see why I like you the best. You're the prettiest." We start laughing again because somehow in the scenario he's become the Cinderella and I've become big balled Prince Charming. God, I'm so tired, but we can't stop laughing.

Sean reaches for my ankle and lifts my foot to his mouth, kissing the pad of my toe lightly. Suddenly, nothing's funny. I gasp as he does it, having no clue that it would make me feel this way.

Sean's lips twist into a wicked smile. "Really? You have a toe thing?"

"I do not." I sound very dignified until he slips one of my toes between his lips and all the air is sucked from my body in a luscious breath. His tongue flicks against my skin and I nearly scream with excitement. Hands clutching the sheets, I sit upright and try to pull my foot away. "No, no, no!"

Sean holds onto my ankle firmly, refusing to free me. "I think the words that you're looking for are, *yes yes yes.* This is so much better than the box. I can see the look on your face, the way your eyes sparkle, the way your lips twist into a panicked smile. Meanwhile, you're the one talking about morality, what's weird and what's not, and then you swoon over toe kisses."

"I'm not swooning." Okay so that's a total lie. As soon as he puts his mouth on my toes again, I'm lost. I'm gone, swept away the same as when he kisses that spot on my shoulder, and I just can't stand it. I moan too loudly and rip the bedding underneath. My nails actually dig into the silk sheets and tear them. My back arches up in the air as I moan with ecstasy.

Sean doesn't relent. His kisses stay focused on my feet, on my toes, until I admit that I have a thing—a very weird super sensitivity where kisses feel good on my toes. The sensations make me writhe and call out. I beg him to stop, but he won't, not until I give in and admit that I'm a foot freak.

In a voice that's way too high pitched and breathy, I dart upright, gasping, "Fine! You're right! You're right." I pant the last word because he's stopped torturing me. I'm such a nutter. I wiggle my foot, trying to jerk it away, but Sean holds on.

He gently massages my toes, touching the right places to make me quiver. Then I'm treated to a full smile that reveals both dimples. "I love it when I'm right."

Chapter 11

The rest of the night flies by in a blissful blur. This is unreal, unlike anything Sean's ever done before. I wonder if this is the man that used to be or if this is a totally new version of Sean that he doesn't know, that no one knows. I'm elated and exhausted, lying naked in his bed. There's a sliver of moonlight peering through the draperies. It feels like I have anvils tied to my eyelashes and every time I blink it becomes harder and harder to reopen my eyes, but I don't want to take my gaze off of Sean.

He's been falling in and out of sleep for an hour now, maybe more. There's a peaceful look on his face that makes me want to watch him, but it also makes me worry. In this state, he's frail. Vulnerability isn't something that equates to Sean Ferro, but there are times when I see it. The most common is at the cemetery when he's standing in front of his wife's grave and looking at the family he lost. He blames himself and he always will.

The thing is, tonight was different than other times because his walls never went back up. It's what I always wanted. It's also what scares the tar out of me. I finally had a taste of what the real Sean Ferro is like, of the beautiful man that lies beneath the torment, and I love him even more. The little traces of who he is that have popped out from time to time are nothing compared to the man I saw tonight.

I want to close my eyes and wake up next to him every day. I want things to stay like this, and have it be me and him against the world. Isn't that what marriage is all about? Forming an alliance with someone, trusting them, hoping they'll be there when you fall, and helping them up when they need you. Sean's afraid of repeating his mistakes and I see that, but he's in this constant state of looking backwards and living in the past.

I was like that. I wanted to be like him. I wanted to be numb to the world and everything in it. I didn't want to feel the pain of losing my parents, but it meant that I gave up feeling anything at all. I don't think I can live that way very long, because what's the point of living if you can't feel?

All the things that I love most are sensations—the breeze on my face, the crunch of fall leaves under my feet, the sand between my toes, and even the warmth of Sean's skin on mine—they're all things I feel. The things I don't want to be without. I wonder if tonight will convince Sean to let go of his past, at least a little, enough to step forward into the light. The only way I'll find out is if I close my eyes and fall asleep. I'm excited to know what tomorrow brings but I'm afraid of it at the same time.

My eyelids close slowly as my gaze is fixated on Sean's lips. To my surprise, his blue eyes are suddenly revealed through dark lashes. A smile twitches at his lips and he reaches out, touching my face, dragging his finger along my cheek. The touch makes me shiver and feel safe at the same time. It's like being touched with ice and fire, and there's no other way to describe it. Both ecstasy and agony.

Sean says sleepily, "Close your eyes spray start car girl. I'll still be here in the morning, nothing will change."

I'm afraid to ask, but I do, "How can you be so sure?"

"Because I finally found what I'm looking for, I was just too stupid to see it." He smiles sleepily at me. "I've made promises before, but I didn't know what I was promising. Now I do. I want this. Every day. Every night. Us. Together, if you'll have me. And if not, I may just wear my man ring and just tell people I'm engaged to the awesome Avery Stanz."

That last remark makes me giggle, I can't help it. Sean caresses my cheek again and I snuggle closer to him. "Was that a proposal, Mr. Jones? Because I believe it's tacky to propose after sex, at least for your kind."

He smirks. "My kind?"

"Yes, your kind—the fabulously wealthy, powerful, and slightly crazy, Ferro family. I'm sure they'd be horrified to learn of such a tacky proposal." I'm teasing him and too sleepy to make up much of a jeer.

He knows it. Sean snuggles closer so we're nose to nose, and he's gazing sleepily at me. "So should we open a condom and put it on my finger as a ring?"

Sean's response is nonverbal, he leans in closer, putting his hands on my side, and tickles me. "The guy who gives you a condom as an engagement ring is a fucktard."

I gasp, opening my mouth like I'm in super shock. "Did you just use slang? Oh my God, I think I might die. The great Sean Ferro sounds like a normal person." I laugh as he tickles me more, but I'm honestly too tired to fight him off.

"This is an extension of the first proposal, which was done correctly and very romantically. You know how hard it was to find someone at the State Park Department to let me rent the damn room? I was on hold for nearly three hours."

Now I tickle him, pressing my fingers into his sides and wiggling. Sean laughs and confesses, "Okay, so it was two hours, but still took forever. That was the proposal. This is the affirmation, the statement that comes later that states I still mean what I said. I want you now, and I want you forever, for the ups, downs, and everything in between. I want you here next to me, like this, every night. I want to kiss you awake every morning. I want to do very dirty things that I will not say out loud, Miss Smith."

I can't help it, I'm smiling like an idiot. I want to believe him. I want to believe it, but he's said this before. Except last time his actions were different. Aren't actions supposed to speak louder than words? I should accept this change, shouldn't I?

With a quiet voice, I say, "I'll have to think about that, Mr. Ferro." I shrug, teasingly.

With all seriousness in his voice, Sean leans on and says softly, "I'll make it right. I promise, I'll be here in the morning." He knows what's weighing on me, what's tugging at my heart, and keeping me awake.

I open my mouth, but it's gone dry, so I nod. I roll over on my pillow the other way, not wanting him to see the emotion that's playing across my face. Hope this high shatters when it falls, it'll break me and I know it. At the same time, I feel like it's a risk I have to take.

People change and grow, and Sean Ferro is not immune to growth. In the limited time I've known him, I've seen him try. I know how hard he fights his demons and his past. I also know there's no reason for him to do that alone. In a lot of ways, we're the same, holding back the past like an inky tidal wave that threatens to crush us at any moment. Two people holding it back should be better than one.

Sean's voice scatters my thoughts when he speaks. "Go to bed, spray start car girl. We can talk about anything and everything in the morning. The only other person in the house is one of the security guards, and he's not stupid enough to come in here, not after seeing you in the foyer with sticks and leaves in your hair. If I didn't know better, I would've thought you concocted a plan to break through my defenses and pull every heart string I have. Apparently, all it takes is a few scratches on your face and messy hair."

"Nope, no concocting. I'm a dumbass and actually ran all this way. I jumped fences in a single bound," I say dramatically, "and fell flat on my face. The result was epic bruising, blisters, and a sore butt. I really don't land on my feet very often." I smile a little bit as I feel Sean snuggle up behind me.

He wraps his arms around me and whispers in my ear, "You don't have to worry anymore. When you jump, I'll catch you. You don't have to land on your feet, not if I'm here."

His words make me smile and that's the last thing I remember before drifting off. The world is still, and warm, and perfect.

Chapter 12

Sean's phone rings, again, stealing him from sleep. I've been lying in his arms half awake, thinking. I don't like this plan. Marrying Trystan does throw everyone off, and I understand why Sean wants to do it— I even understand why Trystan agreed to it—but it's not fair. It's not fair to me and it's not fair to Trystan and it's not fair to Sean. The three of us are living life in limbo, waiting for the other shoe to fall. Going back to the Cinderella thing, I kinda wish the other slipper would just break.

The phone falls silent once again as Sean snuggles into me tighter. I can feel his warm breath over my shoulder and his strong arms around my waist. It's something I've always wanted, a night with him without pain or regret, and a morning with no remorse. I'm not sure if he'll give up his old ways and I'm not sure if I want him to. To tell the truth, I was disappointed we didn't go into his little sex room. I was wondering what kinds of things he would have in there.

Learning how to love and be loved is hard, especially after so much loss. That's something we both know.

The phone rings again, chirping next to my head on the nightstand. I finally lean over to look at it and see who's calling Sean at this hour, and what I see surprises me.

MASTERSON

I wiggle out of Sean's embrace just enough to reach the phone and answer the call. "Marty?"

"Avery? Is that you?" His voice sounds weird, almost panicky.

"Yeah. Why are you calling Sean in the middle of the night?" The pit of my stomach drops. Something's off.

"I can't believe he fucking did this. You aren't supposed to be there—"

I interrupt, "I know, but—"

He cuts me off. "There's no time for it—we're not arguing. Get Sean up and get out of that house now. I shouldn't even be calling, there's no time. Give the phone to Sean."

I don't understand what he's talking about, but the tone of his voice makes me worry. I push up on my elbow and look back at a sleeping, weary, Sean. "Is this about me marrying Trystan? Because I didn't marry him last night, it's an epically bad plan. I was going to —"

He cuts me off again, his urgency even more pronounced this time. Marty's practically shouting into the phone. "Avery, get Sean up now. They know, they're coming for you."

By now Sean's heard me talking to someone and is half awake. "Who is it?" I don't answer, I just hand him the phone.

He's quiet as he listens to Marty explain something. Sean makes very little movement and remains expressionless as he listens. The two of them are far from friends, but add in the common goal of protecting me and they seem like old buddies. Sean pushes up on his elbow, pulling away from me as he does so. "That can't be."

The way Sean says it sends a chill up my spine. His voice is tight. It reminds me of the times he bought me, to help control the world around him. I'm losing the sweetness, the softness of this man, and I don't know why. Sean sits up suddenly and glances over at me. His words with Marty are curt and it seems like they're arguing about something. My heart's racing and I have a horrible feeling in the pit of my stomach, but I just sit there.

"Sean? What's going on?" My question goes unanswered as he angrily nods, listening to whatever Marty has to say.

"And they're coming here? He'd be out of his fucking mind, even if he is who he says. The security detail on the property exceeds anything they'd be able to get through. Why do you think I let her stay here all night? I'm not chancing it with her. This is the safest place until we can formalize things with Trystan. We both agreed to it, Masterson."

Sean goes quiet and I can hear Marty's voice buzzing on the other end of the phone. Whatever he says is absolutely horrific because Sean's face turns white as it goes completely slack. He turns slowly, looking at me as if I'm a ghost.

Now I'm majorly creeped out and done with this. I swipe the phone out of his hand while Sean is still in a daze. "Marty, I swear to God I'm going to," I don't get to tell what I'm going to do with him because he hangs up on me.

Sean bounces out of bed and puts on a shirt quickly. He flies over the bed to the wall's intercom button, but no one answers. Normally it buzzes once and then someone replies quickly, but not this time.

"Jacob? Are you there? Come in." Sean drops his hand from the intercom and swears under his breath. Slowly, he walks toward me and it's as if time has stopped. Ice drips down my spine with the look that he bestows on me.

"We need to get out. Now." Sean doesn't wait for me to answer. He quickly dresses, leaving me stunned sitting in his bed. When I don't move, he comes over to get me. "Come on, Avery, now."

Sean takes hold of my arm, pulling me out of bed, and tosses clothes at me. Not a loving gesture, and the way he's acting is totally freaking me out. "Sean, tell me what's going on."

But he doesn't. Sean races into the other room and grabs the letters that were my mothers. I follow him, pulling on clothes, still asking for explanations that he doesn't give. Sean sifts through the papers quickly, looking for something. When he finds it, he stops and looks up at me. His jaw drops and his lips part, and he just stares. I recognize the look. It's a bad look. It's the *my cat just fell in a trash compactor* look *and I accidentally slapped the button on.*

"Tell me. Whatever it is, I'm going to think it's a million times worse if you don't." I pull the rest of the clothes on and manage to put on my shoes. I'm dressed, but Sean hesitates. He doesn't move. He doesn't grab my hand and take me running the way that it felt like he would. Marty kept saying get out. I don't understand why we're running or who we're running from. I thought the running was over.

I prompt him, "Sean?"

"It will be fine." Sean crosses the room in three long strides and reaches for me, pulling me into his chest and holding me tight. He kisses the top of my head and says, "I won't let them hurt you." He holds me like that and in those moments it's everything I ever wanted. Sean feels like home. He's the home I lost, the home I dreamed I'd one day have when I was a girl. There's a promise of protection in the way his arms wrap around me like nothing can hurt me, and it doesn't go unnoticed. It plays off some carnal need that's buried deep within, but his actions bring it to the surface.

"Sean, you have to tell me what's going on. We're in this together now, remember? Both of us. I'm not leaving you. You can say what you want, but I'm not going to marry Trystan. I want to be with you. I've always wanted you."

Sean's lips part and the words pour out, melting my heart. "I've always wanted you too."

"It's time to act like a team then. Marty didn't tell me crap and you're white as a sheet."

"We need to get to the car. From the looks of it, the house is empty. Either my mother gave everyone the night off or someone else chased them off. Probably the latter, since the head of my security team isn't answering. Either way, it appears that security at the Ferro mansion has been breached. We're not safe, we need to move."

"Okay."

Sean grabs my hand firmly. "We stay together."

Part of me wants to smile and spin around with glee. He wants me with him. The other part of me is terrified because whatever happens next is a complete unknown. The Ferro mansion has security like Fort Knox. The intercom was quiet and whatever Marty said has Sean scared, and anything that scares Sean Ferro must be terrifying.

Chapter 13

We run through the empty house quietly and carefully, not seeing anyone. Sean leaves the lights off, allowing us to slowly slink down the hallway in the darkness. Every time we come to a doorway he makes me stop and holds out his arm, keeping me back until he knows the coast is clear. Then he waves me forward and we continue on like that.

We head toward a back exit, one that's rarely used. It lets out on the far side of the house where Peter leaves his motorcycles from when he was younger. My heart is thumping in my chest, making it feel like my ribs will crack. Hysteria's building in my throat, because it feels like someone's watching us. My skin prickles with the sensation that something horrible's about to happen. Something is very wrong, that much I know. I thought it was strange, not seeing anyone. Sean doesn't usually answer the door. He has a butler that does that. I ask him about it.

Sean looks troubled, but replies, "He went with my mother on her business trip. Someone else would've grabbed the door, but I saw you coming. I looked out the window. Plus, I may have, sort of, kind of, put a GPS tracker on your things." The way he says it is so sheepish that it makes my insides melt, at least after the initial flair of rage.

"Technology hates me."

Sean leads us down a bunch of hallways, we've twisted around the mansion so many times. I don't know where the hell we are.

Sean glances at me out of the corner of his eye, as he releases my wrist. We've come to a set of double doors made from thick, dark, wood. They're elegantly carved, but not as ornate as Sean's. He released my wrist so we can pound on the doors.

Sean's phone rings in his pocket. He lifts it to his ear and listens, then says, "It's just us. No, Pete's at Sidney's and Jon is God knows where, but he's not here. It's just us. Yeah, bikes. Take the back way out of here and we'll meet up with you." They say a few more words and Sean disconnects.

"No one else is here?" I ask, confused. "How can that be?"

"Between business and pleasure most of the family is usually away. I wouldn't come here either, but I thought there was a remote chance you might show up, so I came. We need to move. This is a lot more complicated." Sean looks over at me and takes my hand, pulling me through the grouping of rooms that looks like one of the Ferro boys' residences. There are books scattered about, and posh, manly finishes on the walls.

Before we know it, we're at a small door. Sean shoves through and in a second we're outside in the crisp morning air. Marty is standing there, as is a girl that I've not seen before. She's my height and weight, wearing leather jacket. Long brown hair flows down her back. Marty tosses a set of keys to Sean. There are a pair of motorcycles parked right by the back door.

Marty watches me carefully. "Are you ready to go? I'm going to take her out the front route, you guys go the other way. With the helmets and leather, in the early morning sun, maybe they won't be able to tell it's not you."

This is wrong, it's so incredibly wrong. Shivers take hold of me and I can't shake it off. I pull my hand away from Sean's, demanding an explanation. "You have to tell me. What's going on? Why are they still chasing us?"

Sean's chest expands as he sucks in a short breath and glances down at his hands. Our fingers are intertwined, his hand holding mine.

He looks back at Marty, who gives a visual no. "Don't say it." Marty looks over at me with so much empathy in his eyes, I can't stand it. I don't know how anything could possibly be this wrong, but whatever Sean wants to tell me is important. "Sean, we need to go."

But Sean remains glancing at his hand that's holding mine. "The reason why Campone wanted those papers had little to do with the ledger. There was something else in there, something else that your mother was hiding. It meant enough to her that she spent her entire life running and looking over her shoulder. She knew he'd find her one day, and take back what was his. The ledgers were a cover, and the reason why you attracted so much attention. It became less obvious when Campone died. I thought they wanted me. It wasn't until Marty shed light on things that I realized what we were really up against."

My throat is dry but I managed to ask, "What do you mean?"

Marty interrupts, "Don't—"

But Sean doesn't listen. "During the reading of Campone's last will and testament, your name came up."

I stare at Sean, gaping. "What? Why would I be in his will? That doesn't make any sense. I don't understand what you're saying? The ledgers make sense, but not this. You're saying they want me."

The two of them seem to understand something that I don't. Marty waves his hands over his face and groans as he turns around. The woman standing with him says nothing, although I can tell she cares about him.

Sean swallows hard and looks down at our hands. He turns toward me and says the last thing that I expect to hear. "Victor Campone was your father."

"No, I don't believe you." I pull my hand away from his, trying to back up, but Sean won't let go.

"That's why he showed up." Sean explains, jabbing his thumb at Marty. "That's how Campone's men know for certain—it was in his will. It was also made known that Victor had more than one child. You have a brother that's hunting you. He doesn't want to share Victor's assets. Things turned on their heads overnight. Victor Junior's in charge of Campone's men. The ledgers we have will give us some leverage, assuming we can get out of here before whatever happens, happens. Marty knows that there is a bomb that is supposed to go off around sunrise. They wanted all the Ferros to be in the house, but it just so happened that everyone is away. They thought you would come here because of me. That was part of the reason why I wanted to make the separation between the two of us. We need to move."

I can't move though. I feel like I've been sucker punched and my legs are failing me. They buckle under and I start to go down. Sean reaches for me and holds me up, smashing me into his chest, hugging me hard. I ramble, protesting, "That can't be. I can't be his kid, that's wrong. I look like my father. Everyone said growing up that I look like my father. They didn't mean Victor Campone, they meant my dad. Sean, Marty's wrong, he has to be wrong."

Marty and Sean look at each other, and then back at me. I can't fathom this, even the suggestion of being that man's daughter, having his blood running through my veins, makes me sick. Being hunted for it, that it's the kind of family I came from, and that it's the kind of woman I'm becoming. It scares the hell out of me. Sean takes hold of my shoulders and pushes the hair back from my face. Looking into my eyes, he says, "You are who you are. Your father doesn't matter. We need to go, and I'll be there for you, no matter what."

Marty takes action before Sean does. He tosses a leather jacket to Sean and another to me. "Come on, let's go." Marty puts the key in the ignition and turns it over.

Sean bounces his motorcycle and turns the engine over before nodding at me to jump on the back. I swing my leg over and hop up. I wrap my arms around his waist. It brings back memories of the night we first met, of me jumping on the back of his old bike as we chased my crappy car down Deer Park Ave. "This will out run anything. Hold on tight and don't fall off." I nod, mortified.

"Split up. Let's go as far from here as possible. Head to Oak Island. It's a pain in the ass to get to, but we can hide the bikes in the shrubs and take a boat across the water to get there before it's breakfast time. No one will see us. I think it's the best bet. The only variable is Black. She's still random, a wildcard." The other woman mounts the back of Marty's bike, and pulls on the helmet, fastening the strap under her chin. When she pulls down the visor, the tinting obscures her face and it becomes difficult to tell us apart.

We all do the same, and get ready to drive away. Marty kicks his bike into gear and flies down the driveway, turning in front of the house to take the main road out of here. Sean kicks his bike into gear and revs his engine, ready to fly out of here when his phone rings. The Bluetooth inside his helmet automatically picks up.

"It is far too early in the day to have to deal with those annoying toys."

It's Constance. Sean remains frozen in place. He replies, "Mother, where are you?"

Just as she is about to reply, a deafening sound comes from the back of the mansion. The unmistakable sound of glass exploding and landing on cement fills our ears. A few moments later, a second explosion rocks the mansion, crumbling the walls outside of Sean's rooms. The area we were just in a few minutes ago is engulfed in smoke. Shrapnel is flying everywhere, as wood splinters and metal torques. There's a third blast and the front door explodes outward.

Sean and I stare unable to move, wide-eyed. We both heard it, we both know—Constance is still inside.

SNEAK PEAK:

LIFE BEFORE DAMAGED

THE PRESENT
~PETER~

Sidney nervously twists her engagement ring on her finger and looks up at me. In that soft voice, the one she uses when she's worried, she asks, "What'd you find?"

The pit of my stomach has been in freefall all day, ever since I opened that last box. It was hers—Gina's. After everything we went through, I never realized Gina kept a journal, an account of everything, including vivid descriptions of the man I once was. Sidney knows about my reputation, but what was printed in the tabloids and what's written in these diaries are two very different stories.

It's strange being in love again. I thought I'd die alone. After I lost Gina, I had no aspirations, no hope. Then Sidney changed my life. Holding these books makes me feel my old self, still there, buried deep within. All the rage, the fights, the never-ending line of women who would do anything to fuck me— in these pages, the memories are vivid. As each remembered moment blurs by, I feel the impact, the void of who I was screaming out from deep within. But that period of my life is over, lost to the past, and I force the echoes of who I was to be quiet once more.

Truth be told, I don't miss that life, but I worry about what will happen when Sidney discovers who I was, what I was. Sidney thinks the best of me. She sees me as the English professor, the poet. But deep within, I'm not him. This part of my past lurks within me still. It reared its ugly head when Sidney's ex tried to hurt her. I made him pay for that.

My violence was justified, but it doesn't matter. At the end of the day—even though I changed my name—I'm still Pete Ferro.

Glancing at the journals in my hands, I make the choice. She needs to know. If Sidney is marrying me, she needs to see the good and the bad. Reading it from a tabloid isn't enough. Swallowing hard, I cross the room clutching the books tightly.

I look around the little house Sean gave us, thinking, yet again, how perfect it is—right down to the custom made perch for Mr. Turkey. Sean acts so stoic that I think he doesn't give a shit about anyone or anything, then he does something like this. I can't figure him out. When I see Sean and think of his life, I wonder how similar we really are; I wonder if the only reason that I'm different is because I pretend to be.

Is that all it takes to change? Maybe I'm not different after all, maybe I just want to be. A different last name, a different life—one that isn't etched with scars and faded dreams. When I look at Sidney I feel alive again. The

ghost of who I was disappears and I'm real—
every wish, every dream able to come true
and it's all because of her. Showing these
journals to her could destroy us, but hearing
the truth about me from someone else would
be so much worse. I won't take that chance.

Sidney is sitting on the bed, solemnly
waiting for me to speak, as if she can sense
the weight on my soul. I'd thought my soul
was irretrievably lost until Sidney sat down at
my table and flashed that beautiful smile.
Thank God for her.

"Sidney?" Although I try, I can't hide my
feelings from her, I never could.

"Peter, what is it?"

I sit down facing her, making the bed dip
beneath my weight, and place the books on
the comforter between us. "While I was going
through my old things, I found these—
they're Gina's journals." My voice catches
and I look everywhere except at Sidney.
Sucking in air, I push through. I need to say
this before the hole in my chest consumes
me. It's growing, adding pressure that wasn't

there a moment ago. It scolds me, urging silence.

She won't understand, a voice says in the back of my mind. It latches onto times that I tried to tell the truth and it bit me on the ass. Ice forms, freezing my skin from the inside out, until I shiver.

Sidney places her palm on my hand. It's warm and steady, firm and fragile. She looks up at me with those dark eyes and I want to melt into her. I want to shove these in the trash and run, but I can't. No matter how hard I try, I can't change who I was—who I am.

She has to know.

I manage a half-smile as I look down at her. "While I was unpacking, I found a few old boxes that I never opened after the last move. They were relics from an old life, a past that I didn't want to remember." I pause, trying to muster the strength to say the rest and hand over the books. My jaw tightens as if my body knows this is the fastest way to kill our relationship, but my heart protests. It speaks, forcing the words over my lips, "When I opened it today, I found these books. They're Gina's journals."

Sidney's mouth drops, forming a little O, as a whirlwind of emotions play across her face. Her grip on my hand tightens as she leans in. "Oh, my God. Peter, I'm so sorry. That must have been hard." She reaches forward, taking my other hand, trying to comfort me, but that's the last thing I want right now.

Tipping her head to mine, our foreheads touch. I still, holding her hands, breathing her in, allowing myself to get intoxicated with her scent—her touch. A smile plays on her lips and one of her hands reaches around my neck. She rests her wrist on my shoulder while her fingers play with the hair at the nape of my neck. It's a Sidney motion of kindness, something that makes me want to pull her to my chest and never let go.

Ever since she found out that I was a Ferro, and about Gina, she's been nothing but kind. With the upcoming wedding, Sidney didn't even ask me to drop Gina's last name. She would take it if I asked her to, I know she would. Sidney understands loss in a way that many can't. That's why withholding this part of my life from her isn't right. I don't deserve her.

This is my chance, I know it. It could backfire horribly, and yet, it feels right. Pulling back, I shove my hands through my hair and let out a rush of air. "The thing is, these diaries are about me, about who I was before we met. The guy in the papers doesn't hold a torch to the asshole I used to be, and Sidney, he's still here." Leaning in toward the books, I tap one of the covers. "This guy is still part of me."

From the look on her face, I know she doesn't believe me. It's not that she thinks I'm lying, but it's compassion and forgiveness given unknowingly. I take her hand and absently toy with the stone on her ring. "This is something that you need to know. I'm not the man I was before, but he's still here, buried inside. Asking you to read these is strange, I know. It has the thoughts of another woman and—"

Sidney reaches out, stands, and places a finger on my lips. My heart aches so badly it feels like it may explode. "Shhh. Peter, you aren't the guy you were before. Anyone can see that. Hell, even Sean can see that and he's an asshole." She drops her hand and offers a small smile. "Everyone has a past, even me. We don't have to do this."

"Your past is different. You didn't willingly, knowingly do bad things. I did. If you're going to marry me, if you want to truly be with me and understand my shadows, my faults, and help me from slipping back into the man I was, you need to read these."

My stomach twists into knots saying this to her. There's a million different ways she could take this new information, and I have no idea how much detail Gina went into about how I treated her, what she saw, and what I did. I couldn't bring myself to read more than a few pages. Each one was about how messed up I was and how much she hated me. I was cruel to her, and there was no reason, no excuse. Gina painted me as the perfect storm, glorious to behold and equally deadly, destroying everything in its path without remorse or shame.

Sidney takes the first book and nods. "I'd do anything for you Peter, but no matter what's in here, it won't change my mind about you, about us."

"I wouldn't be too sure about that." Stepping back quickly, I shove my hands in my pockets and dart out of the room before she can respond.

~LIFE BEFORE DAMAGED
is on sale now~

COMING SOON

The Arrangement 19

*****

To ensure you don't miss H.M. Ward's next book, text AWESOMEBOOKS (one word) to 22828 and you will get an email reminder on release day.

*****

Want to talk to other fans?
Go to *Facebook* and join the discussion!

MORE FERRO FAMILY BOOKS

NICK FERRO
~THE WEDDING CONTRACT~
*****

BRYAN FERRO
~THE PROPOSITION~
*****

SEAN FERRO
~THE ARRANGEMENT~
******

PETER FERRO GRANZ
~DAMAGED~
******

JONATHAN FERRO
~STRIPPED~
******

MORE ROMANCE BY H.M. WARD

SCANDALOUS

SCANDALOUS 2

SECRETS

THE SECRET LIFE OF TRYSTAN SCOTT

DEMON KISSED

CHRISTMAS KISSES

SECOND CHANCES

And more.

To see a full book list, please visit:
www.sexyawesomebooks.com/#!/BOOKS

CAN'T WAIT FOR H.M. WARD'S NEXT STEAMY BOOK?

★★★★★

Let her know by leaving stars and telling her what you liked about
THE ARRANGEMENT 18
in a review!

COVER REVEAL:

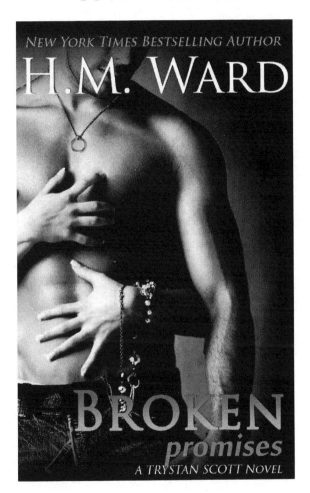

NEW YORK TIMES BESTSELLING AUTHOR

H.M. WARD

BROKEN
promises

A TRYSTAN SCOTT NOVEL

Made in the USA
San Bernardino, CA
24 August 2015